D0187736

THE SKY'S THE LIMIT!

Adapted by Ellie O'Ryan

Based on the series created by Dan Povenmire & Jeff "Swampy" Marsh

Disney PRESS

New York

Printed in the United States of America
First Edition
10 9 8 7 6 5 4 3 2 1
V475-2873-0-12341

Library of Congress Control Number: 2012941072
ISBN 978-1-4231-4907-1

For more Disney Press fun, visit www.disneybooks.com
Visit DisneyChannel.com

Part
ONE

Phineas and Ferb plunked two big bowls, filled to the brim with their favorite cereal, on the coffee table. It was early in the morning, and sunlight filled the living room. The brothers were just about to eat breakfast before heading outside for a fun day of summer activities.

"Nothing starts off a day better than

3

some breakfast and some education," Phineas said as he turned on the television.

The television screen glowed and an announcer started speaking. "We now return to *Wacky Millionaires in History!*" it said excitedly.

An old black and white photo of a man with slicked-back hair and a thin moustache flashed onto the screen. The show's narrator

explained that the man was named Howard Hughes and that he was famous for being a successful businessman as well as for building incredible airplanes.

"Howard Hughes is probably best known for building the *Spruce Goose,* so-called because of its wooden frame," the narrator said.

Another old photo popped up. This one was of an enormous, old-fashioned airplane. "With a wingspan of three hundred nineteen feet, eleven inches, it still holds the record for being the largest plane ever built," the narrator stated officially.

Phineas perked up as he watched an old video of the *Spruce Goose* flying through the air. "Wow, that's an impressive record!" Phineas exclaimed. "Three hundred nineteen feet, eleven inches is just over the length of a football field. And it's only one afternoon

away from being broken. Ferb, I know what we're gonna do today!"

At the start of the summer, Phineas and Ferb had pledged to make the most of their vacation by filling every single day with fun and adventure. From traveling on exotic trips to building astonishing inventions, the brothers spent all their free time making sure that each day was as amazing as possible! They knew how lucky they were that Phineas's mom and Ferb's dad had gotten married, making the boys stepbrothers *and* best friends. And neither one wanted to waste a moment of summer vacation. So when one of the brothers had a great idea, the other one was sure to be on board!

Ferb understood exactly what Phineas had in mind. In fact, he had guessed that Phineas would want to break the airplane record the moment the *Spruce Goose* image had come onto the screen. So Ferb had put on a black wig and a tiny moustache for the occasion. With the costume, he looked just like the famous Howard Hughes!

Phineas and Ferb went right to work. First they piled old newspapers in the backyard. Then they gathered several large bags of flour. Just then, Isabella, Buford, Baljeet, and the Fireside Girls stopped by.

"Hey, guys," Isabella called out. "What'cha doin'?"

"We're making the biggest airplane ever!" Phineas replied.

"Cool," Isabella said. "Coincidentally, we're going for our aeronautics patches."

Phineas nodded. "Coincidentally," he said, "we could use extra hands."

"Coincidentally, we're in!" Isabella exclaimed happily.

Phineas grinned. With this many helpers, they were sure to break the record in no time!

"We're making our plane out of paper-mâché with newspaper," Phineas explained to his friends.

"Why? To make sure it's *newsworthy*?" Isabella joked. Everyone laughed.

"And *read* all over!" Phineas added, making everybody laugh again.

"Oh, oh, oh. And *funny*!" Buford chimed in.

Everyone grew silent and stared at him.

"You know, 'cause—'cause—the funnies," Buford tried to explain his joke. He held up the comics page of the newspaper. But his friends still didn't laugh.

A moment later, Phineas broke the silence. "Seriously," he said, "Howard Hughes called his plane the *Spruce*

Goose because it was made of wood. So we're going to call ours the *Paper Pelican* because it's made out of newspaper. You know, so it'll have a good *circulation!*"

Once more, everyone cracked up . . . except for Buford.

"Aw, come on!" Buford complained. He thought his joke had been twice as funny as Phineas's, but no one had laughed at it.

Suddenly, Phineas looked around. "Hey, where's Perry?" he asked.

The brothers glanced around the yard, but their pet platypus, Perry, was nowhere to be seen. What Phineas and Ferb didn't know was that behind their pet's disguise as a normal platypus, Perry was actually a secret agent! Called Agent P by his fellow operatives, he worked undercover for O.W.C.A., or Organization Without a Cool Acronym. His nemesis, the evil Dr. Doofenshmirtz, was always up to some sort of diabolical scheme that Agent P needed to stop. Agent P had a secret lair hidden beneath Phineas and Ferb's house that he could access at any time. And that was just where he was headed now!

Agent P snuck over to a flower bed on the other side of the house. Then, without so much as a sideways glance, he pushed down on one of the flowers. The entire flower bed flipped over, sending him straight into his underground lair.

A moment later, Agent P was seated in front

of a flat-screen monitor where his boss, Major Monogram, waited to deliver a briefing.

"Ah, Agent P," the major began in his gruff voice. "We've just discovered Doofenshmirtz has been stealing bottles from recycling bins. And nothing good can come from that." An image of Dr. Doofenshmirtz digging through a trash can appeared on the screen next to Major Monogram.

"Unless, of course, he's recycling, in which case nothing *but* good could come from that," Major Monogram continued. Then he frowned. "Unless he's recycling it into some hideous weapon, which is something, once again, no good could come from. Except, of course, for the recycling part, which I guess is still, at its essence, good. Even if you're making something evil, it's still recycling . . ." The major paused and scratched his head. "You know, perhaps we shouldn't even put these 'good' and 'evil' labels on things. Let's just say Doofenshmirtz is doing something neutral. Get out there and make sure it stays like that."

Agent P didn't need to be told twice. His captain's chair flipped around again, and Agent P ran off to begin his mission.

Good, evil, neutral . . . it didn't matter to Agent P. He was determined to get to the bottom of Dr. Doofenshmirtz's strange new obsession with digging through trash cans.

And Agent P wasn't afraid to get his hands dirty!

Back in Phineas and Ferb's yard, the group had been hard at work all morning constructing an enormous wire frame for their airplane. Once the frame was finished, it was time to start making the paper-mâché. A huge conveyor belt chugged along, mixing flour with water until it had turned into a goopy, gloppy paste. Ferb stood next to the conveyor belt and used a shovel to keep the paste flowing. One by one, Fireside Girls dipped buckets into the gooey mixture and carried the paste over to the airplane frame.

Baljeet was in charge of making sure they had enough newspaper to cover the entire plane. He scoured the neighborhood for every spare newspaper he could collect. He even yanked the morning news right out of the hands of Phineas and Ferb's father as Mr.

Flynn-Fletcher drank his morning coffee! Then Baljeet delivered the newspapers to the Fireside Girls.

Isabella and her troop carefully tore each sheet into long, thin strips. They passed the strips to one another, dipping them in the buckets of paste and sending them up a ladder where Phineas and Ferb slapped them onto the wire airplane frame. Piece by piece, the paper-mâché plane was coming together.

Soon it would be ready to take to the sky!

Unaware of Phineas and Ferb's high-flying activities, Agent P arrived at the headquarters of Doofenshmirtz Evil, Incorporated. He activated a hidden panel on the wall of the building, which spun him right into the middle of the evil scientist's lair.

"Perry the Platypus!" Dr. Doofenshmirtz gasped. The evil doctor moved into a fighting stance, ready to face off with his nemesis.

Suddenly, a phone on the table next to the doctor rang. Dr. Doofenshmirtz picked up the receiver. "Hello?" he said. Then he held the receiver out to Agent P. "It's for you, Perry the Platypus."

Agent P walked over to Dr. Doofenshmirtz warily, his eyes narrowed. He had reason to be suspicious. As soon as he was close enough, Dr. Doofenshmirtz sprang into action. He wrapped the twisty telephone cord tightly around the secret-agent platypus. In an instant, Agent P was completely tied up!

"Ha, ha!" Dr. Doofenshmirtz laughed evilly. "Prank call!"

Dr. Doofenshmirtz didn't waste much time gloating. He was too excited about unveiling his latest invention.

"Now, say hello to my new evil weapon," he told Agent P. "My Evaporator-inator! It's made completely out of recycled materials. It's green"—Dr. Doofenshmirtz paused to pull open his lab coat so that he could show Agent P his T-shirt with the recycling logo—"and evil. I call it *greevil*!"

Agent P looked at the Evaporator-inator, which had been strategically placed in front of several large windows. It was made almost entirely out of clear glass bottles and seemed to be one of Dr. Doofenshmirtz's stranger inventions. The bottles were arranged in a circular pattern and held together by a thick purple band.

"Backstory time!" the doctor cackled. He

closed his eyes as he thought back to a memory from his childhood. "You see, Perry the Platypus, when I was a young boy, my mother would never let me swim in public pools." He remembered the days well, when dressed in a striped, one-piece bathing suit, he would stand sadly by the edge of a swimming pool, watching all the other kids splash and play in the water. His mother would just look at him with a stern expression and tell him, "No."

Agent P waited expectantly to hear the rest of the story. After a moment, he realized that was the end of Dr. Doofenshmirtz's flashback.

"What?" the evil doctor asked with a shrug. "You know, not every backstory has to have some big in-depth spiel, Mr. High Expectations!"

Agent P didn't disagree. But he still needed to know what Dr. Doofenshmirtz planned to do with his Evaporator-inator. Every snippet of information could help him uncover the evil genius's latest scheme. No detail was too insignificant . . . and Agent P wanted to learn them all.

Chapter
THREE

Meanwhile, Candace and her best friend, Stacy, were on their way to a pool party at Jeremy's house. Candace was superexcited. She'd had a crush on Jeremy for a long time, and she couldn't imagine a better way to spend a beautiful summer day than hanging out at a pool party with him. She had even picked out a special bathing suit for the occasion. It was pink with a white flower on the front.

As Candace and Stacy approached Jeremy's house, Stacy held her arm in front of Candace. "Wait . . ." Stacy said. She stared at her watch for a few seconds, then nodded. "*Now!* We're *exactly* fashionably late."

The girls crossed the street and walked through the gate into Jeremy's backyard. "We're here!" Stacy announced. Then she turned to Candace and smiled. "This is going to be so cool."

Just then, Candace spotted something.

Jeremy was sitting on the side of the pool, dangling his feet in the water. And he wasn't alone. A beautiful girl with blonde hair was sitting next to him. She was wearing the exact same bathing suit as Candace! But what worried Candace most of all was the way Jeremy seemed to be laughing and smiling as he chatted with the girl.

"That is *so* cool!" The sound of Jeremy's voice carried over the pool to where Candace stood, as he responded to something the mysterious blonde girl had said.

"Who's that Jeremy's talking to?" Candace asked Stacy.

"I have no idea." Stacy shrugged. "I've never seen her before in my life."

The friends dropped down to their knees so that no one could overhear their conversation. They began crawling across the patio.

"I thought Jeremy invited me to this party," Candace said anxiously.

"Let's not jump to conclusions yet," Stacy said. They popped up behind two lawn chairs to get a better view.

"What is he doing with her?" Candace demanded. She was so confused.

"Slow down." Stacy tried to calm her friend. "You remember that time you thought Jeremy was with a girl and she wasn't even a *she*? And then you ended up on that snowboard all crazy and out of control?"

"Yeah," Candace admitted. She sighed. "But *she's* obviously a real girl," Candace added, pointing to the mysterious blonde.

The friends peeked out from their hiding place so they could overhear Jeremy's conversation with the blonde girl.

"So then I've got two West African pit vipers, and I had to dive off a three-hundred-foot cliff and swim up through a school of piranha!" the girl said in a charming Australian accent.

Jeremy was captivated by her exciting story. "That's awesome, Nicolette!" he exclaimed.

Candace gasped. "Stacy, it's conclusion-jumping-to time!" she exclaimed. "Strategy session, *now*!"

Candace grabbed Stacy's arm and dragged her through a tall hedge so that they could talk privately.

"She's *amazing*!" Candace wailed. "She's all exotic and stuff. She has on the same

bathing suit as me, only it's brighter and she wears it better. And she dives off cliffs holding poisonous snakes, into piranha-infested water. What am I going to do? She's like catnip for boys. She's *boynip!*"

Stacy listened sympathetically. It wasn't unusual for Candace to get upset when she saw Jeremy paying attention to another girl. Stacy knew that her job, as Candace's best friend, was to reassure her . . . and try to keep her from overreacting. After all, just because Jeremy was hanging out with a girl didn't mean that he had stopped liking Candace.

But Stacy had to admit, Nicolette's long list of daring feats was going to be a tough act for Candace to follow!

Chapter FOUR

In Phineas and Ferb's backyard, the boys and their friends gazed up proudly at their airplane. The *Paper Pelican* was finished— and it looked awesome!

"Nicely done, people," Phineas said. "Hey, Baljeet—what are the stats on the *Spruce Goose* again?"

"The *Spruce Goose*'s wingspan is three

hundred nineteen feet, eleven inches," reported Baljeet.

"And the *Paper Pelican*'s wingspan is . . . ?" Phineas asked.

"Three hundred twenty feet even!" Baljeet announced grandly.

"Eat your heart out, Howard Hughes!" Phineas cheered.

The *Paper Pelican* really was an enormous airplane. Its wheels and undercarriage barely fit onto the empty lot next to Phineas and Ferb's house, let alone the backyard. The plane's wings, tail, and nose stretched across the entire block, casting long shadows over all the neighbors.

The moment of truth had arrived. It was time for the *Paper Pelican*'s first takeoff! Phineas and Ferb went to invite all the neighborhood kids for a flight they would never forget. Meanwhile, Baljeet and Isabella cheerfully volunteered to be head flight attendants. They changed into crisp, brightly colored uniforms and stood next to the *Paper Pelican*'s boarding staircase as the passengers began to climb on.

"Welcome aboard!" Isabella and Baljeet said in unison.

Buford walked up to the staircase and narrowed his eyes at Baljeet. "You'd better have some decent grub on this bucket," he said. As the resident bully of Danville, Buford was always looking for something—or someone—to pick on.

Baljeet just smiled. "You will be most gratified," he promised. Buford grunted and stomped up the clanking stairs. Once he was

out of earshot, Baljeet tapped his fingers together nervously. "As long as you find insignificant bags of peanuts gratifying," he said. He already knew that Buford would *not* be happy . . . and Baljeet was afraid of what that would lead to. "Welcome to Wedgieville, population me," he mumbled.

Once the last passenger had climbed aboard, Phineas and Ferb jumped into the cockpit. They wore vintage flight gear, including sheepskin coats, pilots' caps, and thick goggles—just like Howard Hughes wore when he flew the *Spruce Goose*.

"All right, Ferb, let's go through our preflight checklist," Phineas said as they took their seats. He swiveled in his chair to inspect the control panel. It was crowded with dials, levers, and gauges. "Pilot's instruments? Check," he said.

Phineas turned to Ferb. "Copilot's instruments?" he asked.

Ferb gestured at the side of the cockpit where a guitar, a trumpet, a tambourine, a harmonica, and a drum kit were safely stashed. "Check!" Ferb replied.

"Looks like everything's a 'go,' Ferb," Phineas said happily. "Let's switch her on. Ignition!"

Phineas reached up to push a blue button over his head. The plane's engines roared to life and eight propellers started to spin.

"Adjust angle of departure. Check," Phineas said as he began working the plane's controls. The nose of the plane lifted up . . . and then it started to fly!

Soon the *Paper Pelican* was soaring high above the city of Danville. Phineas glanced out the window. All the houses looked so tiny! The noisy whir from all the propellers was deafening, but Phineas wasn't nervous. He felt just like the famous Howard Hughes! He reached over and pressed the intercom button on the control panel. "We've reached cruising altitude," he announced. "You are now free to move about the cabin."

Isabella jumped out of her seat and grabbed a silver tray that was piled high with tiny snack packets. "Would you like some peanuts?" she politely asked one of her friends.

"I'll take two!" the girl replied.

Across the aisle, Baljeet approached Buford with a similar tray. Buford's eyes narrowed before Baljeet had even reached him. "That had better not be insignificant bags of peanuts," Buford growled.

Baljeet immediately hid the tray behind his

back. "No, of course not, sir," he stammered. He laughed nervously and darted away.

A moment later, Baljeet returned and presented Buford with an unusual dish. It looked like a roasted chicken . . . but it was made entirely out of peanuts! There were torn peanut packages scattered around the platter like a garnish. Baljeet could only hope that Buford wouldn't realize that there wasn't any *actual* chicken in this delicacy!

"Here, sir, try our deluxe peanut chicken," Baljeet said. "Our motto is, 'So peanutty, you will not even taste the chicken!'"

"I'd better not taste any chicken then, loser!" Buford snapped. He ripped off a drumstick and jammed it in his mouth. After crunching loudly, Buford swallowed. "All right," he said, satisfied. "You survive . . . for now."

"Oh, thank you, sir," Baljeet said gratefully. He was sure that if he could keep the *Paper Pelican*'s most difficult passenger happy, the airplane's first flight would be a big success!

While all the passengers were nibbling on their peanuts, Baljeet and Isabella went to the front of the plane. They stood before a royal blue velvet curtain. "And now, for your in-flight entertainment," they announced. "The *Paper Pelican* floor show!"

Together, Isabella and Baljeet drew back the curtain to reveal the Fireside Girls standing in a long row. One by one, the girls stepped aside until Ferb was left alone at center stage. He had changed into a white dinner jacket, and his green hair was slicked back in an old-fashioned style, just like Howard Hughes! And he was wearing the small moustache again. Ferb began singing a smooth fifties' song that sounded like something his grand-parents would have listened to on the radio decades ago. The catchy tune was truly the perfect accompaniment for the Fireside Girls' amazing show!

Dressed in matching flight-attendant uniforms, the girls climbed into a pyramid formation on top of the *Paper Pelican*. They kept perfect balance as the plane soared through the air. But the acrobatics didn't stop there! The Fireside Girls flipped and turned, changing the pyramid's shape over and over. Finally, they grabbed one another's hands and, defying gravity, formed a wide circle that was big enough for several smaller airplanes to fly through!

The astonishing air show was the most high-flying fun that Phineas and their friends had ever seen. Phineas grinned at his brother. This adventure in the wild blue yonder was unlike anything they had done all summer. And Phineas was pretty sure even the famous Howard Hughes would have been impressed.

Back at Jeremy's house, Candace sat on the grass with her head down. Stacy knew that it was time for a pep talk . . . a *serious* pep talk.

"What are you worrying about?" Stacy said encouragingly. "You're Candace Flynn!"

"Yeah," Candace moaned. She pointed over at Nicolette. "And *she's* supercool, foreign accent, snake wrestler, high-diving, natural hottie Nicolette!"

"Snake wrestler? Whatever," Stacy said with a dismissive wave of her hand. "You've fought dinosaurs. You've been to Mars. You've traveled through time!"

"Oh, yeah," Candace realized.

"And as for diving, you've been perfecting that quintuple-somersault-backflip-jackknife-swan-dive for a week now," Stacy reminded Candace. "You're Candace Flynn!"

"Yeah!" Candace exclaimed. She was so inspired that she burst through the hedge and yelled, "I'm Candace Flynn!"

"Candace?" Jeremy asked in surprise, turning around. He turned away from Nicolette.

"Oh," Candace said coolly. "He remembers my name. How nice."

Candace strode off to the pool without giving Jeremy a second glance. She was pumped. She was psyched. She was Candace Flynn . . . and she was ready to do something really extraordinary!

Candace climbed onto the diving board and cleared her throat so that everyone would

pay attention to her. "Ahem! There's been a lot of talk around here about diving and snakes and diving with snakes into pools filled with piranhas and sulfuric acid," she said loudly. She shot a look in Nicolette's direction.

"I didn't say anything about sulfuric acid," Nicolette spoke up.

"Leave all questions 'til the end of the rant. Thank you," Candace said. This was it—her moment. She was going to show everyone, including Jeremy, an incredible dive that would leave them speechless.

But Candace had no way of knowing that across town, Dr. Doofenshmirtz's Evaporator-inator was about to put a serious hitch in her carefully devised plan.

At Doofenshmirtz Evil, Incorporated, the doctor laughed maniacally at Agent P. "Now say good-bye to splashy pool-time fun . . . forever!" he cried.

Just before firing up the Evaporator-inator,

Dr. Doofenshmirtz pointed to one of the machine's special features. "Even my power source is *greevil*," he bragged. "Look, look, it's solar!"

Agent P didn't have a moment to lose. While the doctor was distracted with starting up the machine, he escaped from the telephone cord wrapped around him and stood in a martial arts pose facing Dr. Doofenshmirtz.

"Huh? Seriously?" the doctor said in

disbelief. Before he could say another word, Agent P took a flying leap and kicked Dr. Doofenshmirtz in the chin! The evil scientist stumbled backward, right into the Evaporator-inator's power button. The machine trembled. Then, harnessing the energy of the bright summer sun, it shot a green beam right into downtown Danville—and Jeremy's backyard!

At the pool party, Candace was ready for her big moment. "Now, as I was saying before I was so *lamely* interrupted," she began, bouncing on the diving board, "I'm going to show everybody a real daredevil dive!"

Zzzzzzzzzaaaaaaaaaaaappppppppppp! Just as she was about to jump, the beam from the Evaporator-inator hit Jeremy's pool. The water disappeared instantly!

"That's just not fair!" Candace complained.

She was the only one who was disappointed, though. The rest of the partygoers immediately grabbed their helmets and skateboards.

"Hey, cool, it's like a half-pipe!" one of them yelled.

"All right!" cheered Jeremy. Then he led several skateboarders into the empty pool so that they could show off their best stunts.

"No, wait! No—argh!" Candace groaned from the diving board. "I've been practicing diving, not skateboarding! Everyone stop doing things I'm not good at."

Just then, Jeremy toppled off his skateboard. And while he slid to a halt at the bottom of the pool, his skateboard continued up the side, landing on the very edge of the pool. Candace didn't see it as she stormed away from the diving board. "Oh, this is a nightmare," she grumbled. "Come on, Stacy, let's—ahhhhhhhhhhhhhhhhhhhhh!"

Candace accidentally stepped onto Jeremy's skateboard. Then she zipped down the side of the pool!

She rolled in a half-pipe along the pool and reached the other edge. A boy quickly jumped

up and put a helmet on her head. "Safety first!" he shouted.

Whoosh! Candace rocketed back across the half-pipe, where another kid slapped elbow pads onto her arms. "Safety first!" he repeated.

But Candace was too busy to notice. She was screaming at the top of her lungs! Her skateboard bounced off the diving board, soared through the air, and skidded down the roof of Jeremy's house. Candace gritted her teeth and covered her eyes as she zoomed down a tree branch before landing on the diving board again. This time, Candace and the skateboard flew straight up in the air, doing a series of spins and flips.

"Wow, Candace!" Jeremy exclaimed as he watched. He was clearly impressed.

But little did Jeremy know he would soon be a part of Candace's crazy ride!

Up on the roof of Doofenshmirtz Evil, Incorporated, Agent P continued to battle his nemesis. He used a series of skilled martial arts moves to grab Dr. Doofenshmirtz's arm and fling him across the roof.

Unfortunately for Agent P, the evil doctor landed right next to the Evaporator-inator. His eyes lit up.

"That was your last highly improbable judo maneuver, Perry the Platypus!" Dr.

Doofenshmirtz cackled. "I will now evaporate you into nonexistence!"

Dr. Doofenshmirtz swiveled the Evaporator-inator around and pointed it directly at Agent P. The machine started to hum and glow with solar energy.

Agent P was just about to duck for cover when out of nowhere, all three hundred twenty feet of the *Paper Pelican* airplane flew overhead. It completely blocked the sun! The plane's shadow fell across the roof. Without solar power to fuel it, the Evaporator-inator stopped working.

"No! My—my power source!" Dr. Doofenshmirtz exclaimed. "Oh, great, now I can't see a thing."

Agent P leaped into action, taking full advantage of the sudden darkness.

Wham! It took just one well-timed karate kick to send Dr. Doofenshmirtz flying over the edge of the roof.

"Curse you, Perry the Platypus!" the evil doctor howled as he fell. It was a long way to the bottom of Doofenshmirtz Evil, Incorporated. Luckily for the doctor, he'd experienced this fall many times before. There was always a spare clothesline for him to grab onto or an open window for him to crawl through somewhere along the way. Still, Dr. Doofenshmirtz was disappointed. His latest evil scheme hadn't turned out nearly as *greevil* as he'd planned. Next time, he'd have to come up with something even more clever to outwit his nemesis.

On the roof, Agent P straightened his fedora, pleased with the outcome of yet another successful mission. But he didn't linger long. With the Tri-State Area safe once again, he had to get back to Phineas and Ferb's house before they noticed he was missing!

Across town, the crowd at Jeremy's pool party was cheering wildly for Candace's gravity-defying skateboard stunts. Even Candace couldn't believe her luck! She'd bounced from the diving board, to the roof, to a tree limb, and now she was skateboarding along the entire rim of the pool. She was starting to wonder if she was good at skateboarding after all.

Just then, the *Paper Pelican* flew over Jeremy's backyard. Its enormous shadow blocked the sun, and all the partygoers looked up in surprise at the darkness.

"I can't see!" Candace screamed in a panic.

"Candace?" Jeremy called from the bottom of the empty pool.

Whack!

Without any sunlight to help her see where she was going, Candace crashed into Jeremy at top speed! No one knew exactly what had happened until the plane flew away, letting the sun shine down on the pool again. Candace and Jeremy were tangled at the bottom of the pool, dazed from the collision.

"At least she had that airbag," somebody commented.

"That's got to hurt," another guy added.

The kids knew that there was only one thing to do: call Candace's mom.

After spending many hours at the hospital, Mrs. Flynn-Fletcher finally drove Candace and Jeremy home. "Well, every day is eventful in the emergency room, Candace," her mom said. "You really should be more careful."

"Mom, I told you, we had our helmets on," Candace replied as she struggled to open the car door with a heavy cast on her arm. Then she held the door open for Jeremy, who was on crutches. Candace watched as Jeremy climbed out of the car. She agreed with her mom that the emergency room was no fun. However, there *had* been a plus side to the unexpected hospital trip. It had given Candace a chance to talk with Jeremy in the waiting room. And she'd learned all about the mysterious girl named Nicolette. "So your *cousin* Nicolette was trapped on a video game level?" Candace

said to Jeremy with a small smile as they walked to the house.

"Yeah, it took her a week to get through," Jeremy said. "You didn't think she really did all those things?"

Candace laughed sheepishly. Then, Jeremy pulled a marker out of his pocket. "Candace?" he asked, pointing at her cast. "Do you mind?"

"Yes," Candace said dreamily. "I mean, no. I mean, sign it."

Jeremy drew a heart on Candace's cast.

Then he wrote their initials, "C + J" inside.

"Thanks." Candace giggled. Though the cast meant she wouldn't be showing off any fancy diving moves for several weeks, as long as Jeremy's heart was on it, Candace didn't mind at all!

High above Danville, the *Paper Pelican* was just finishing its high-flying adventure. Phineas nodded at Ferb and switched on the intercom. "This is your captain speaking," he said. "We're beginning our descent."

"Okay, everyone," Baljeet announced from the middle of the aisle, "please return your seats to the upright position."

With a splash, the *Paper Pelican* made a watery landing in Danville Lake. Then the plane started to come apart!

"And please do not panic," Baljeet added quickly. "As you can see, the *Paper Pelican* is dissolving in water because it is, after all, made

of paper-mâché. But do not worry, because your seat cushions also function as flotation devices. Thank you for flying with us!"

Phineas and Ferb gave each other a thumbs-up as the *Paper Pelican* dissolved into Danville Lake and their seats floated safely to shore. Though they might never be stars on the show *Wacky Millionaires in History*, the brothers were pretty sure their flight was one for the history books.

Just then, another seat popped out of the water . . . with Perry the Platypus floating on top of it! He made his chittering noise loudly to get Phineas's attention.

"Oh, there you are, Perry," Phineas said

with a smile. It seemed even Perry had been in on the high-flying fun!

Breaking a world record, soaring in an airplane, floating across a lake . . .

What a perfect way to spend a summer day!

Part TWO

Phineas and Ferb leaned against a tree in their backyard, enjoying the cool shade of a lazy afternoon. Suddenly, a noise caught their attention.

Thunk! Thwack!

An apple fell out of the tree. It bounced from Ferb's head to Phineas's head before Phineas caught it.

"Ha, gravity," he said, chuckling. Phineas

studied the apple for a moment. "Hmm. I wonder if there's any way around that."

Just then, the boys' older sister, Candace, marched into the backyard. She had dedicated her summer to busting Phineas and Ferb's outrageous plans. And if being their sister had taught her anything, it was that Phineas and Ferb were up to the most trouble when they were sitting under the tree doing absolutely nothing. "What are you guys doing?" she demanded.

"Well, right now we're just thinking of defying gravity," Phineas told her.

"Please," Candace scoffed. "Even you can't change the law of gravity. It's a universal law. Like you can't wear white after Labor Day."

"An absolute law without hope of appeal? That's despotism!" Phineas exclaimed. "Somebody ought to—hey, that's it! I know what we're gonna do today." Just then, he looked around. "Hey, where's Perry?" he asked.

"Right here," Candace replied. She pointed at the ground near Phineas's feet, where their pet platypus, Perry, snoozed.

"Oh," Phineas said. "I didn't see him there."

Phineas and Ferb were used to Perry disappearing for hours on end every day, only to show up later with no explanation. So it was strange that Perry was actually with them in the backyard for a change. Unbeknownst to them, Perry was really a secret agent named Agent P. Normally, on a summer day like today, Agent P would be off on a mission to stop his nemesis, Dr. Doofenshmirtz. But this afternoon seemed quiet. Agent P hadn't been called upon. The warm sunshine was perfect for a nap. And as long as evil was on a break, Perry didn't mind taking some time to relax.

Phineas and Ferb shrugged and raced inside the house. They needed to get started on their latest invention!

A short while later, Ferb put the finishing touches on a complicated-looking schematic and passed it along to his brother. "Hey, Ferb, nice job on the blueprint for our Antigravity Fun Launcher," Phineas exclaimed. He turned to the computer. "I just posted it on our Web site so Baljeet can check the math."

Brrrrring! The phone rang before Phineas could even finish his sentence.

"Hey, Baljeet," Phineas said into the phone. "That was fast."

"Your blueprints are ninety-seven percent accurate," Baljeet said. "But you accidentally placed a cosine where you needed a quadratic differential." He giggled. Mathematical mistakes always made him chuckle! "Not to worry, I fixed it. I will send an attachment."

"Excellent," Phineas replied as he hung up. This lazy summer afternoon was turning into

one of the brothers' best adventures yet. Soon they would have an Antigravity Fun Launcher!

Then they would find out once and for all if the law of gravity could be broken!

Across town at the headquarters of Doofenshmirtz Evil, Incorporated, someone else was looking for a way to spend the day. Agent P's nemesis, Dr. Doofenshmirtz, sighed glumly. "There's absolutely nothing going on today," he complained.

"Have you finished that puzzle yet?" asked Norm, Dr. Doofenshmirtz's robotic assistant.

Dr. Doofenshmirtz looked at the puzzle and frowned. The cheerful image of a rainbow and a smiling sun was complete except for the last five pieces, which were scattered on the table next to the puzzle.

"No," Dr. Doofenshmirtz grumbled. "I lost the stupid box lid, and now I can't figure out how to solve it."

"Then you could finish building me a bride out of icicle-pop sticks like you promised," Norm suggested. He pointed at a half-finished robot made of blue-tinted sticks.

"I'd like to help you out, Norm, really," Dr. Doofenshmirtz said as he walked over to a mirror. "But look at my tongue! See?"

Dr. Doofenshmirtz stuck out his tongue. It was bright blue! "Look at that," Dr. Doofenshmirtz moaned. "My doctor said no

more blue-raspberry icicle-pops until the blue dye flushes completely out of my system."

"Why must I be alone?" Norm asked sadly.

"I don't know. Why are raspberry icicle-pops blue?" Dr. Doofenshmirtz replied. "I really need an evil scheme, but . . . oh, it's so hard to create when I'm in one of my moods." Suddenly, the doctor's eyes lit up. "Maybe I can borrow someone else's plans from the Internet!" he cried.

Dr. Doofenshmirtz sat down at his computer and started browsing the Web. "Blueprints," he mumbled as he typed. "And, search!" He hit the ENTER key, and within moments, he stumbled across Phineas and Ferb's Web site. "Ooh, an Antigravity Fun Launcher!" Dr. Doofenshmirtz exclaimed in delight.

He printed a copy of the plans and grabbed a pencil. Then he scribbled over the blueprints. "How about the Antigravity *Evil Launch-inator*? There. I changed the name. That makes it mine. This could be the greatest scheme ever!" He cackled wickedly.

Then he paused. "Although, I'm not quite sure of the evil applications. Eh, something will come to me."

Dr. Doofenshmirtz smiled as he started plotting ways to use the Antigravity Evil Launch-inator against the Tri-State Area. His boredom was quickly turning around. Perhaps this would turn out to be one of his evilest schemes yet!

Over at the O.W.C.A. headquarters, Carl the intern was taking advantage of the unusual peace and quiet to update his online profiles.

Just as he was typing, Major Monogram walked up behind him holding a clipboard in his hand.

"Carl, I—" Major Monogram began.

"One minute, sir," Carl interrupted. "Just finishing my status update." He turned back to the computer. "Carl is interning like there's no tomorrow," he said as he typed. "Done!"

Major Monogram cleared his throat. "Carl, I

just completed your intern evaluation report," the major said. "You've earned a gold star in every category except one. You need to show more initiative."

Carl stared at the clipboard in disbelief. Sure enough, he had earned gold stars in the columns labeled "Studious" and "Hygiene."

But there was a sad-looking frowny face in the column marked "Initiative."

"Sir," Carl wailed, tears forming in his eyes, "I've never gotten less than a gold star in my entire interning life!"

"Well, I do have twenty-four hours before I have to submit my evaluation," Major Monogram replied. "Prove you can show initiative, and that gold star is yours."

"I'll start right now by triple-checking the Chattersphere for suspicious activities," Carl promised. He jammed a headset over his ears and began typing furiously.

Carl spent the next few hours diligently monitoring the Internet for signs of suspicious activity in the Tri-State Area. Just as he was beginning to think it was a normal summer afternoon after all, his computer's alarm sounded.

Beep! Beep! Beep! Beep! Beep!

Carl scanned the monitor. "Doofenshmirtz just downloaded a blueprint," he exclaimed as he programmed the computer to intercept the transmission. "Antigravity Fun Launcher?" Carl read the name of the file. "Sounds fishy. Let's run it through the Anagram Decoder."

With a few quick keystrokes from Carl, the computer rearranged the letters in the blueprint's name into other possible phrases. When it finished, Carl was shocked by the results. "Major Monogram!" he cried as loudly as he could.

"You don't have to yell. I'm right here," the major replied from beside him.

"Dr. Doofenshmirtz just downloaded these plans for an Antigravity Fun Launcher," Carl reported breathlessly. "But when I run that through the Anagram Decoder, the letters form 'Evil Fanatic Hunt R Raygun!'"

**EVIL FANATIC
HUNT R RAYGUN**

Major Monogram looked at the screen and frowned. "Looks like you're missing an E," he pointed out.

"They're probably just trying to mislead us," Carl said knowingly. "Let's check the source."

Major Monogram and Carl watched as the computer began to trace the file back to its initial upload.

"Agent P's owners!" Carl gasped. "They must be in league with Doofenshmirtz."

Major Monogram shook his head. "I don't know, Carl," he said doubtfully. "Sounds a little far-fetched."

"But wait," Carl said. "Listen to this. It's a seemingly innocent voice recording of Phineas."

Major Monogram listened carefully as Carl played an audio clip of Phineas saying, "Ferb, I know what we're gonna do today!"

Carl's fingers flew across the keyboard. Then he adjusted the settings on the speaker. "But if we play all those syllables backwards in random order," he continued, "we get . . ."

Carl's voice trailed off as he let the recording speak for itself.

"Let's help Doofenshmirtz take over the Tri-State Area," Phineas's garbled voice said through the speakers.

The voice didn't sound anything like

73

Phineas. But the message was enough to worry Major Monogram.

"Keep a close eye on those boys," he told Carl. "See what else you can find out."

Major Monogram went straight to the briefing room. This turn of events had him worried. If Phineas and Ferb *were* working for Dr. Doofenshmirtz, then Agent P's role of fighting evil was compromised. He was too close to the boys. Even though Major Monogram trusted Agent P completely, he couldn't make his top agent choose between his owners and defending the Tri-State Area. Something had to be done.

A short while later, Major Monogram had Carl set up the video camera. He sent an urgent transmission to Agent P's wristwatch communicator. Agent P zoomed to his secret lair for instructions at once.

"Agent P, we need you to track down a missing agent, code name: Agent G," Major

Monogram said over the large monitor. "We're not sure of his current location, but we have a few leads placing him in Iceland; Monte Carlo; Burbank, California; and the moon. It's up to you to chase that goose and bring him back to the agency. Good luck, Agent P. Monogram out." He gave a salute.

The screen crackled with static at the end of the transmission.

But Agent P never wasted a moment when he was assigned a mission. He was already long gone!

Back at main headquarters, Carl turned off the video camera. "So who is Agent G again?" he asked.

"Gary the Gander? Oh, that's just a wild-goose chase. Get it? Goose, gander?" Major Monogram chuckled. "We had to distract Agent P because he's too close to Phineas and Ferb."

"Who will investigate the boys?" Carl asked.

Major Monogram frowned. "Hmm. We need to send someone in undercover. All the agents are out on their missions," he replied.

Then the major glanced down at his trustworthy intern. Carl knew what that look meant. It meant he was going on an undercover mission—all on his own! He was so excited that he clenched his fists together and squealed in delight. "Eeeeeeee!"

This was it—his big chance to show some initiative and get that gold star once and for all!

But first, Carl needed the right undercover disguise. He wouldn't rest until he'd found the perfect one. He tried on lots of different costumes. But none of them would allow Carl to really go unnoticed as he was monitoring Phineas and Ferb. At last, Carl picked the perfect disguise: a white T-shirt, short orange overalls, and a blue baseball cap. He almost looked like a regular kid!

"Good luck, Agent Carl," Major Monogram said as he saluted O.W.C.A.'s newest secret agent.

"You can count on me, sir!" Carl said gleefully as he jumped onto his scooter and zipped off to Phineas and Ferb's house.

When he got there, the boys and their friends had already begun constructing their Antigravity Fun Launcher.

Phineas looked up from the blueprints. "Okay, *now* where's Perry?" he asked as he glanced around the yard.

The platypus was nowhere in sight. Neither Phineas nor Ferb would have believed that at that moment, their very own Perry was scaling Iceland's snowiest mountain in his search for Agent G!

In the backyard, Phineas turned back to the plans. "All right, guys, chop, chop," he said. "Time to prove Sir Isaac Newton wrong."

Carl rode up on his scooter and crouched behind the fence. He whispered into his wrist-watch communicator.

"Sir, I've reached the target. Over," he reported.

Major Monogram's voice crackled over the speaker. "Now observe, then infiltrate."

Carl grabbed his binoculars and peered over the fence.

But he did not go unnoticed.

"Who's that, Phineas?" Isabella asked.

All the other kids turned around to see what she was talking about.

Carl gulped. He'd been spotted!

"Oh, hey, kid," Phineas called out to Carl. "Do you want to help?"

"Sure," Carl replied. Then he whispered into his watch, "Sir, I've made contact."

"Hey, thanks!" Phineas said as Carl walked over. "What's your name?"

Behind his glasses, Carl's eyes went wide.

Say a cool name, like Nitro, Dax, or Steel! he thought. But when he spoke aloud, he said, "My name is Carl."

Phineas shook Carl's hand. "Nice to meet you, Carl. Come and join in the fun."

As soon as Phineas was out of earshot, Carl whispered into his communicator again. "Sir, I've gained their trust."

Carl knew that he had to act natural in order to blend in with the other kids. He rushed over to help Phineas carry a large metal panel across the yard.

"So, what kind of scheme is this?" Carl asked, trying to sound casual.

"We're just having fun challenging universal laws," replied Phineas.

Carl frowned. He decided to approach someone else for more information.

"So I hear you're the math genius behind this operation," he said to Baljeet a little while later as they sawed wood.

Baljeet laughed and waved his hand in the air. "Oh, no, no, no," he said. "Phineas and Ferb's blueprints were already brilliant. I just made a minor modification."

Carl narrowed his eyes. "Interesting," he said slowly.

Next, Carl made his way over to Ferb. "So, Ferb, you don't talk much, do you?" he asked.

"Actually, I—" Ferb began.

But he was immediately interrupted by Carl, who had just noticed something across the yard. "Ooh, what's that over there?" Carl yelled. He ran off to investigate before Ferb could even reply.

With so many kids helping, the Antigravity Fun Launcher was ready in no time. Phineas, Ferb, Carl, and the others stood back to admire their creation. It was a large dome covered with red metal panels. Two tall antennas poked out of the top. The launcher also had a circular porthole and a steel control panel. Ferb held a rectangular remote in both hands. To Carl, it looked very suspicious. He had to

report back to Major Monogram what the boys had created.

Just as he was getting ready to sneak away, Phineas started to speak. "Nice job, everyone," Phineas said. "It came out perfectly. Who wants to go first?"

"I think our guest should go first," Isabella suggested. She patted Carl on the shoulder.

"Me?!" Carl exclaimed. He tapped his fingers together nervously. He was trapped. Now there was no chance for him to report the diabolical machine Phineas and Ferb had invented to Major Monogram.

At least, not before he'd become its first test subject!

FOUR

Carl stared at the scary-looking machine. But with everyone watching him, he knew that he had to test out the Antigravity Fun Launcher. Otherwise, he might blow his cover.

Carl walked cautiously into the machine and tried to smile. The heavy door closed behind him with a loud *clang*.

"Okay, Ferb," Phineas announced as his brother operated the remote control. "Let's see

what we can do about that pesky gravitational pull."

When Ferb turned a knob on the remote, flashes of electricity crackled along the Antigravity Fun Launcher's antennas. Suddenly, Carl was shot up out of a porthole at the top!

"Whoa!" Carl cried. "What's happening?"

"Don't worry, it only lasts fifteen minutes," Phineas called to Carl. Then he turned to the others. "Looks fun, though. Let's all go!"

Everybody cheered and followed Phineas into the Antigravity Fun Launcher. One by

one, they popped up into the air, just like Carl.

The Antigravity Fun Launcher truly lived up to its name. The kids floated weightlessly in the air, turning cartwheels and somersaults high above Phineas and Ferb's backyard. Isabella grabbed Carl by the hands and spun him around. Then, Phineas and Ferb started a game of zero-gravity Frisbee with their friends!

Carl was so confused. "So, what exactly is the evil purpose in all of this?" he asked Phineas. This just seemed like playing!

"Evil?" Phineas repeated. "This is just for fun!"

Carl watched Phineas float across the sky. He caught the Frisbee as Phineas tossed it to him, and stared at it thoughtfully for a moment. Then a huge smile broke across Carl's face. Maybe Phineas and Ferb weren't working for Dr. Doofenshmirtz, after all. "Hey guys, wait for me!" he called.

Just then, Candace came outside. She should have been surprised to see her brothers

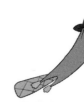

levitating in the air. But at this point, *nothing* they did could surprise her.

"Phineas and Ferb floating in midair?" she asked. "Oooh, they are so busted this time! I've got to find Mom!"

As Candace rushed off to bust her brothers, Carl's wristwatch started to beep.

"Carl? Status update. Over!" Major Monogram's voice barked over the speaker.

"Sir, I can't—" Carl began.

Then Ferb floated over and wrapped a long rope around Carl. When Ferb gave the rope a tug, Carl spun around like a top! "Wheeee— ahhhhhhhhhhhhhhhhhhhhh!" Carl shrieked with glee.

But all Major Monogram heard over his walkie-talkie was the sound of screaming.

"Carl? Carl!" Major Monogram said urgently.

There was no response.

"Oh, no. They must be torturing that poor kid," Major Monogram said anxiously. "Don't worry. Help is on the way!"

The major lifted a striped panel that covered a bright red emergency button on the main computer. This button was no toy. If Major Monogram pressed it, he would immediately mobilize O.W.C.A.'s Emergency Task Force.

Luckily, the agents were equipped to handle themselves in almost any situation, so the button didn't get much use. But Major Monogram felt confident of his decision as he jammed his finger on the button.

If ever there were a time to use the emergency button, it was now!

Meanwhile, outside the headquarters of Doofenshmirtz Evil, Incorporated, the evil doctor's very own Antigravity Evil Launch-inator sparkled in the sunlight. Unfortunately for Dr. Doofenshmirtz, he wasn't aware that he had misunderstood Phineas and Ferb's plans. The Antigravity Fun Launcher's antennas were supposed to stick straight up in the air. But Dr. Doofenshmirtz's Launch-inator was lying on its side.

Dr. Doofenshmirtz turned to Norm. "Thanks for bringing this down for me," he said. "For some reason, it runs on solar power."

But neither Norm nor Dr. Doofenshmirtz noticed that they had parked the Antigravity Evil Launch-inator right next to an enormous "No Parking" sign—until a police car pulled up, lights flashing and siren blaring! An angry cop jumped out of the cruiser.

"How many times do I have to tell you?" the cop asked. "You can't park in a loading zone!"

The officer whipped out his ticket book and started writing.

"Well, now, it—it's not a vehicle, it's an evil device," Dr. Doofenshmirtz stammered. "You see? This is what I do for a living."

But the cop didn't want to hear it. He showed the ticket to Dr. Doofenshmirtz anyway. Then he called a tow truck to haul away the Antigravity Evil Launch-inator.

Dr. Doofenshmirtz ran after the tow truck, howling in outrage. "No, don't, oh!" The first evil device he'd ever built right off the Internet was being hauled away before his very eyes!

Chapter FIVE

Thousands of miles away, in Monte Carlo, Agent P was in the middle of a very high-stakes card game. Dressed in a fancy tuxedo, the platypus sat facing a shady-looking man, also in a tuxedo and wearing an eye patch. Agent P tossed several gold chips into the center pile on the table. The man with the eye patch chuckled. Then he turned over his cards. A pair of aces.

Agent P didn't even flinch. He slapped his cards on the table . . . and revealed a photo of Agent G!

"Gary the Gander?" his opponent cried as the crowd around them gasped. "I know nothing!" the man insisted.

But that wasn't good enough for Agent P. He leaped onto the poker table and tackled the gambler. Everyone in the casino was shocked—but Agent P didn't care.

If anyone in Monte Carlo knew *anything* about Agent G's whereabouts, Agent P was

going to find them and get the information he needed.

No matter what it took!

In Phineas and Ferb's backyard, the effects of the Antigravity Fun Launcher were beginning to wear off. After fifteen free-floating minutes of fun, the force field started to fizzle. Phineas, Ferb, Carl, and the other kids drifted gently to the ground.

"Woo-hoo!" everyone cheered as they landed.

"That was so much fun!" Carl exclaimed. "Remember when Isabella—"

"Ahem!"

Near the fence, someone loudly cleared his throat. All the kids turned around to see who it was. Carl could hardly believe his eyes. It was Major Monogram! He was wearing a neatly pressed pair of khaki pants and a colorful Hawaiian shirt. Carl realized that Major Monogram had gone undercover himself to check on the status of the mission.

"Who's that?" Phineas asked.

Carl looked to Major Monogram for guidance.

"Uh . . . hello . . . son," Major Monogram said awkwardly to Carl.

"Hi, Carl's dad!" the kids said, waving.

"Hello, children," replied Major Monogram. "Carl, your . . . uh . . . mother and I were worried when you didn't come home, uh . . . are you in trouble?"

Carl ran up to him. "No, Major—er—Dad. I was just playing with my new friends." Then, Carl added, "Sir, situation neutralized."

Major Monogram nodded. Then he quickly turned away and spoke into his walkie-talkie. "Abort mission! I repeat, abort mission!"

Little did Phineas, Ferb, and their friends know that more than a dozen stealth helicopters and armored vans from O.W.C.A. were surrounding the house! When Major

Monogram pressed the emergency button, the vehicles had been immediately dispatched on a rescue mission for Carl. All they were waiting for was Major Monogram's signal to launch their rescue operation. But with the major's "abort" command, the vehicles immediately retreated. Phineas and Ferb had no idea how close they'd come to be being arrested by O.W.C.A.!

Back in the yard, Major Monogram nodded at Carl. "Well, uh, son, it's time to go home."

"Aw, come on, *Dad*, can't I just stay for five more minutes?" Carl pleaded. Carl had been so busy interning for the past several months that he was enjoying his afternoon with Phineas, Ferb, and their friends.

Major Monogram clapped his hand on Carl's shoulder. "No, no," he said. "We have to go. Your mom is making dinner."

Phineas and Ferb waved as Major Monogram led Carl out of the backyard. "See you later, Carl! It was a lot of fun!" Phineas called after them. Then he turned to the others. "Nice kid. Last one in has to clean up!"

Everybody laughed and ran for the house, leaving the Antigravity Fun Launcher alone in the backyard.

While the kids clambered inside, a tow truck hauled a very strange device down the road. A few minutes later, a huffing, puffing Dr. Doofenshmirtz came running after it. The doctor was desperate to get his Antigravity Evil Launch-inator back before it was locked up in Danville's impound lot.

"Stop! Stop!" Dr. Doofenshmirtz cried at the top of his lungs. But the tow truck kept speeding down the street, driving way too fast for Dr. Doofenshmirtz to catch up.

Just as Dr. Doofenshmirtz jogged past Phineas and Ferb's house, something in the backyard caught his eye. He could see the silver antennas of their Antigravity Fun Launcher poking above the fence.

"Hmm. That's an interesting shape," he said. "It looks famil—"

Suddenly, Dr. Doofenshmirtz stepped on a

can in the middle of the street. It rolled under his foot, sending him flying through the air. He landed face-first on the pavement with a *thump*.

The evil doctor groaned and rolled over. Then, he saw the Antigravity Fun Launcher from an entirely different angle.

"Wait!" he gasped. "An Antigravity Evil Launch-inator. I've found another one! What are the odds?"

Dr. Doofenshmirtz chuckled and whipped out his cell phone. "Norm! Get down here! I need help!" he cried into the phone.

As Dr. Doofenshmirtz dusted himself off, an evil smile spread across his face. *Two* Antigravity Evil Launch-inators in one day had to be a sign. This scheme was destined to turn out even more diabolical than he'd originally hoped!

Chapter
SIX

After interrogating the man with the eye patch in Monte Carlo, Agent P's mission had led him to sunny Burbank, California. He managed to snag a slot on a talk show where he would ask the host for help locating Agent G. There was just one condition: The host had to keep Agent P's true identity a secret!

The production crew at the TV studio arranged for a blurry, pixilated circle to cover

Agent P's face while he was on the air. This effect made Agent P virtually unrecognizable.

The show's host smiled brightly as the cameras started filming. "Our next guest is a covert secret agent," he said to the viewers at home. "We've pixilated his face to conceal his identity."

Then the host leaned in closer to Agent P. "Now, I understand that you're searching for a long-lost colleague?" he asked.

Agent P handed the host a photo of Agent G.

"Oh," the host said in surprise. "You brought a picture!" He held the photo in front of the camera. "Now, viewers, if you see this agent, call in immediately."

Brrrring!

At that instant, the phone on the host's desk started to ring. Agent P grabbed the receiver, listened intently, and ran off the stage. The caller had given him just the information he needed. All the pieces were falling into place.

Agent P was sure that by the end of the day, he'd track down Garry the Gander and put an end to this wild-goose chase once and for all!

Click-clink-click-clink-click-clink.

Norm extended his metal legs and arms so that he towered over Phineas and Ferb's house. Then he gently reached down and plucked the Antigravity Fun Launcher out of their backyard.

"Norm, you're spectacular!" the evil doctor marveled. "I never knew you could do that."

"Did you know I could also do this?" Norm asked. His metals parts started to rotate and rearrange themselves so that he converted into a pickup truck. The Antigravity Fun Launcher— or the Antigravity Evil Launch-inator, as Dr. Doofenshmirtz called it—was securely stowed in the back of the Norm-truck.

"Wow," Dr. Doofenshmirtz said. "I should really read your instruction book."

"Yes. Yes, you should," agreed Norm.

Dr. Doofenshmirtz climbed into the Norm-truck's cabin. They drove away just as Candace and her mom got home.

Candace could barely contain her excitement. She was *finally* about to bust her brothers!

"It's about thirty feet tall with electrodes and stuff," she said, describing the antigravity machine to her mom.

"Mm-hmm," Mrs. Flynn-Fletcher replied. Somehow, she felt like she'd heard this story before.

"You'll see," Candace said confidently. She leaped out of the car the moment it stopped. "I'll just open the gate and you'll . . . eek!"

Candace was stunned to discover that the backyard was empty. The Antigravity Fun Launcher had disappeared. "It's gone!" she wailed, looking around.

"That's a shocker," her mom said.

Candace looked around desperately, but

the Antigravity Fun Launcher was nowhere to be seen. That's because it was speeding off to the headquarters of Doofenshmirtz Evil, Incorporated!

Dr. Doofenshmirtz laughed maniacally as he steered the Norm-truck. "Norm, you have really outdone yourself today!" he exclaimed.

But the sound of a police siren following them quickly put a stop to Norm's celebration. Dr. Doofenshmirtz groaned as he pulled over to the side of the road. It was the same cop from earlier that day.

"You got a license to drive a robot with more than two axles?" the police officer asked.

"Uh . . . hmm" he stammered.

"That's what I thought," the cop said as he started writing out another expensive ticket. "Okay, Charlie, pull 'er up!"

Beep! Beep! Beep!

A tow truck started to back up, using its strong hook to snag one of the axles.

"Curse you, motor vehicle code!" Dr. Doofenshmirtz howled as the tow truck dragged him off. In just one day, he had lost *two* Antigravity Evil Launch-inators. And what did he get in return? A one-way ticket to the impound lot.

Perhaps today wasn't destined to be the evil success Dr. Doofenshmirtz thought it would be, after all.

Later that afternoon, at O.W.C.A. headquarters, Major Monogram called Carl into the

main briefing room. "I'm very proud of you," Major Monogram said. "But my feelings can better be expressed in this evaluation."

Major Monogram handed Carl the revised evaluation. A shiny gold star sparkled in every category—including "Initiative"!

"All gold stars!" Carl cried in delight.

Major Monogram smiled proudly. Carl had done well on his first undercover operation. It was good to know he could count on his intern when he needed to.

Suddenly, a tremendous crash thundered

through the room. Major Monogram and Carl turned to find that a hole had been blasted right through the wall! As soon as the smoke cleared, Agent P stepped through the hole. He was wearing an orange space suit with a clear plastic bubble over his head.

"Oh, there you are, Agent P," Major Monogram said. "Sorry about the wild-goose chase. You were just too close to this case. But don't feel bad. No one could ever find Agent G. He's been missing for far, far too long."

Agent P frowned. Then he pulled his hands out from behind his back and pushed a grumpy-looking goose toward Major Monogram. Agent P really *had* found Agent G! The wayward goose, wearing a flowery lei around his neck, did not seem happy to be back at work.

"What the—Agent G!" exclaimed Major Monogram. He was shocked! "On an *extremely* extended vacation, hmm?"

Major Monogram removed the lei from

Agent G's neck and slipped it over Agent P's helmet. "Well, Agent P deserves a vacation more than *you* do," Major Monogram told the goose.

Then the major turned to Agent P. "He deserves one, but, unfortunately, evil never rests, so we'll see you tomorrow," he said with a shrug. Then he saluted his top agent.

Agent P didn't salute back. He gave Major Monogram a long, hard stare.

"Well, this is getting a little awkward," Major Monogram said.

But Agent P still wouldn't return the salute.

"Carl, my arm is getting tired and he won't salute back," said Major Monogram.

Carl just nodded. There was nothing he could do about that, really. Carl might make a great undercover agent. But when it came down to it, no one was better than Agent P!